THERE WAS A COLD LADY WHO SWALLOWED SOME SNOW!

by Lucille Colandro
Illustrated by Jared Lee

SCHOLASTIC INC.

New York   Toronto   London   Auckland   Sydney
Mexico City   New Delhi   Hong Kong   Buenos Aires

With love to all the cousins.
—L.C.

For Maya Duke Dietrich
—J.L.

ISBN-13: 978-0-439-47109-1
ISBN-10: 0-439-47109-5

50   17 18 19 20/0

Printed in the U.S.A   40

First printing, February 2003

There was a cold lady who swallowed some snow.
I don't know why she swallowed some snow.
Perhaps you know.

There was a cold lady
who swallowed a pipe.

She wasn't the type
to gulp down a pipe!

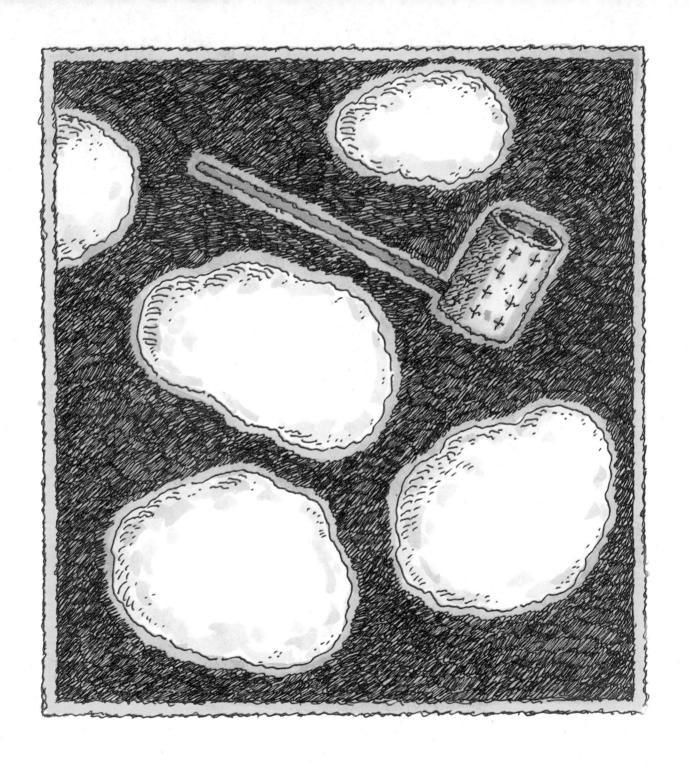

She swallowed the pipe to warm her ten toes
that tickled and tingled from layers of snow.

I don't know why she swallowed some snow.
Perhaps you know.

CRUNCH
CRUNCH

There was a cold lady
who swallowed some coal.

What was her goal
when she gobbled the coal?

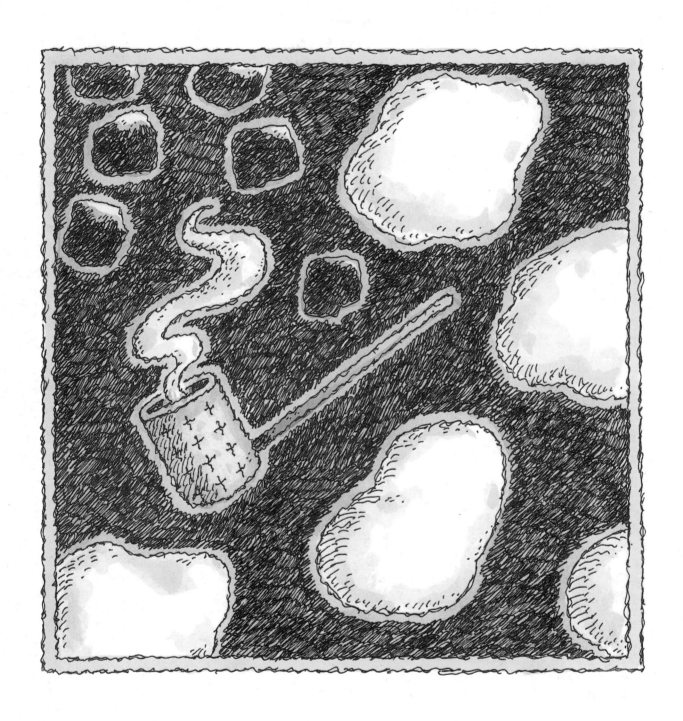

She swallowed the coal to keep her pipe's glow.
She swallowed the pipe to warm her ten toes
that tickled and tingled from layers of snow.

I don't know why she swallowed some snow.
Perhaps you know.

There was a cold lady
who swallowed a hat.

Imagine that—
a black-brimmed hat.

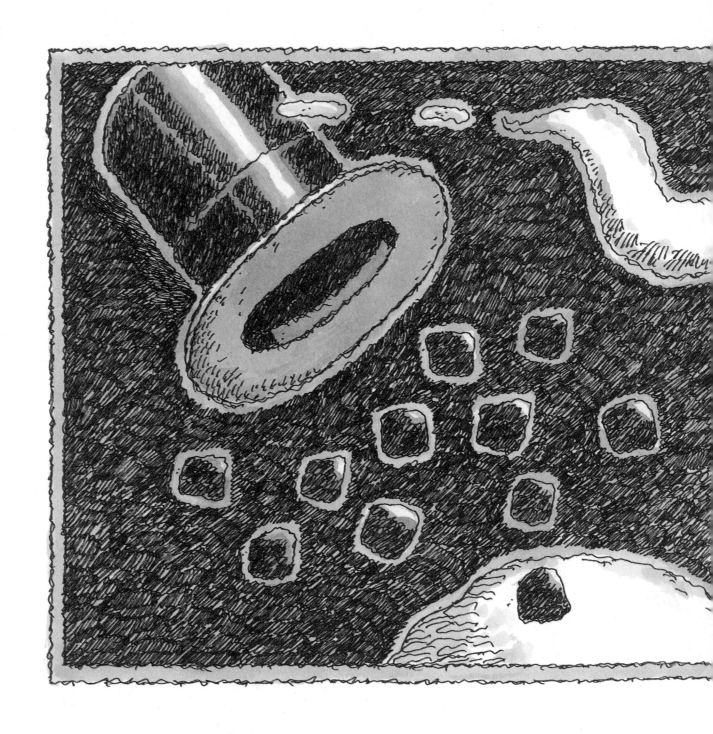

She swallowed the hat before she froze.
She swallowed the coal to keep her pipe's glow.

CRACK

There was a cold lady
who swallowed a stick,
a long, brown branch—
what a pick!

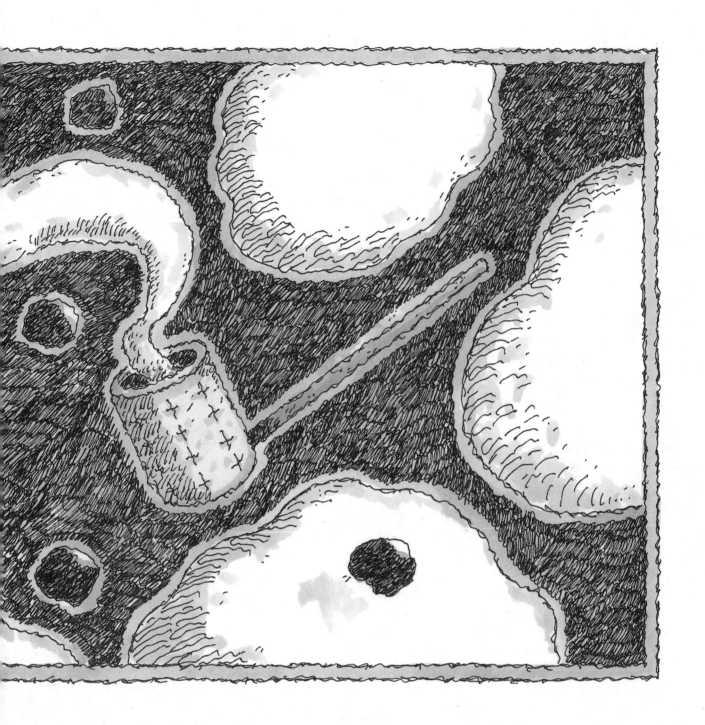

She swallowed the pipe to warm her ten toes
that tickled and tingled from layers of snow.
I don't know why she swallowed some snow.
Perhaps you know.

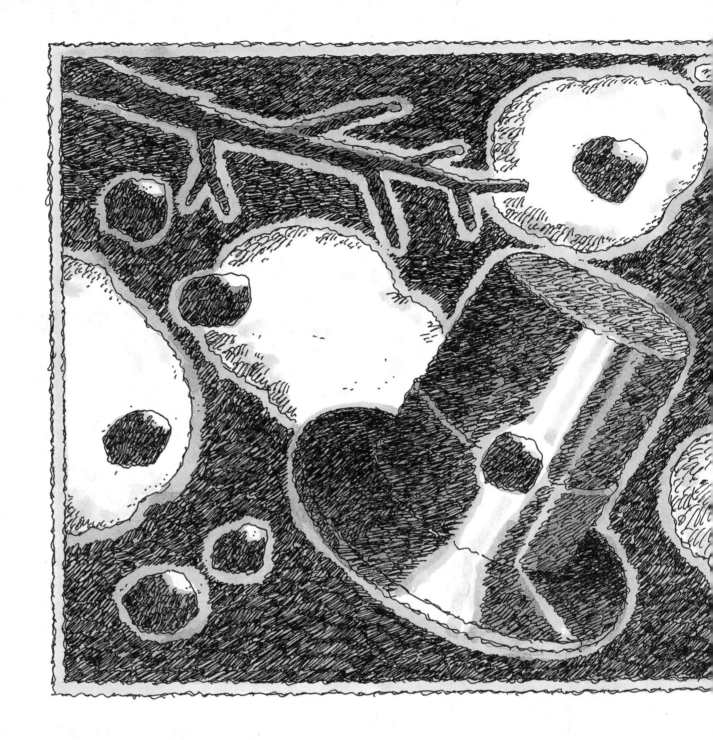

She swallowed the stick to push down the snow.
She swallowed the hat before she froze.
She swallowed the coal to keep her pipe's glow.

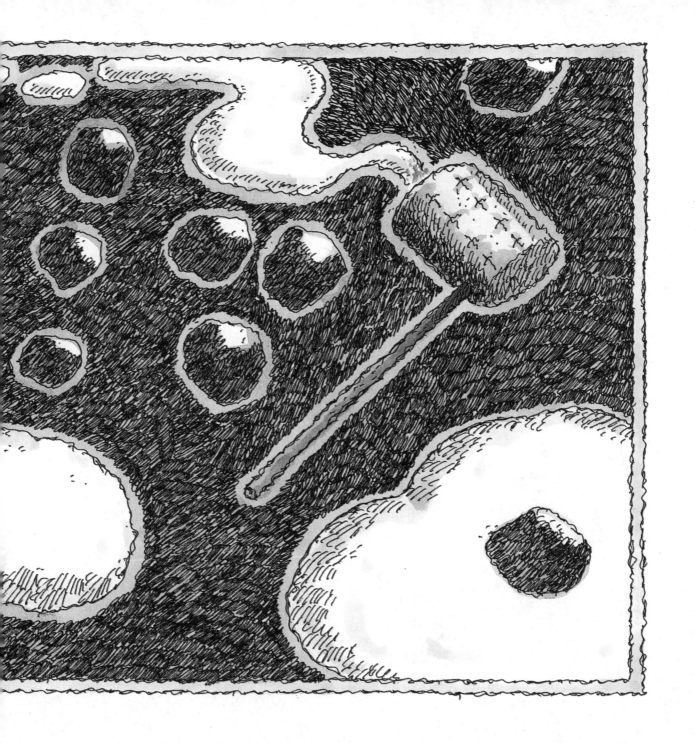

She swallowed the pipe to warm her ten toes
that tickled and tingled from layers of snow.
I don't know why she swallowed some snow.
Perhaps you know.

There was a cold lady who swallowed a scarf,
a long, striped scarf.
She tried not to barf.

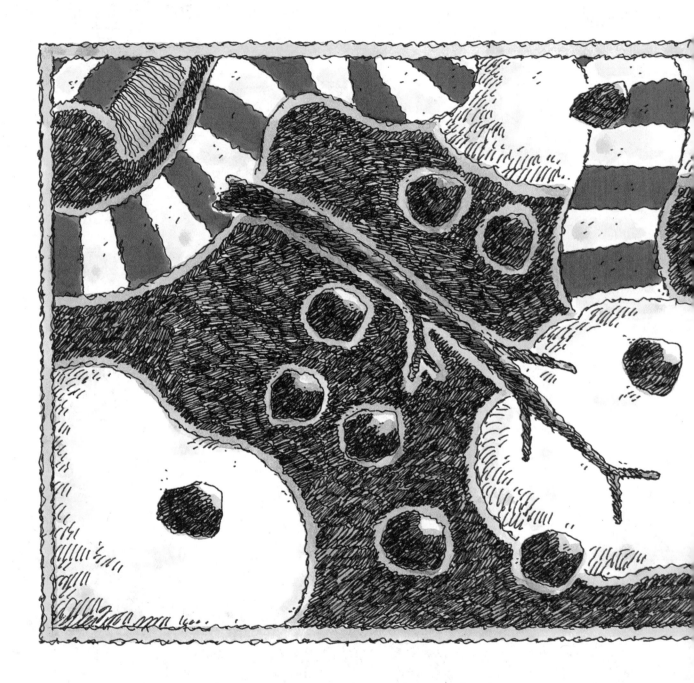

She swallowed the scarf 'cause it was so cold.
She swallowed the stick to push down the snow.
She swallowed the hat before she froze.
She swallowed the coal to keep her pipe's glow.

She swallowed the pipe to warm her ten toes
that tickled and tingled from layers of snow.
I don't know why she swallowed some snow.
Perhaps you know.

now, this cold lady had quite enough!
So, she thought and she thought
and came up with a plan.

She hiccupped twice and
out popped...

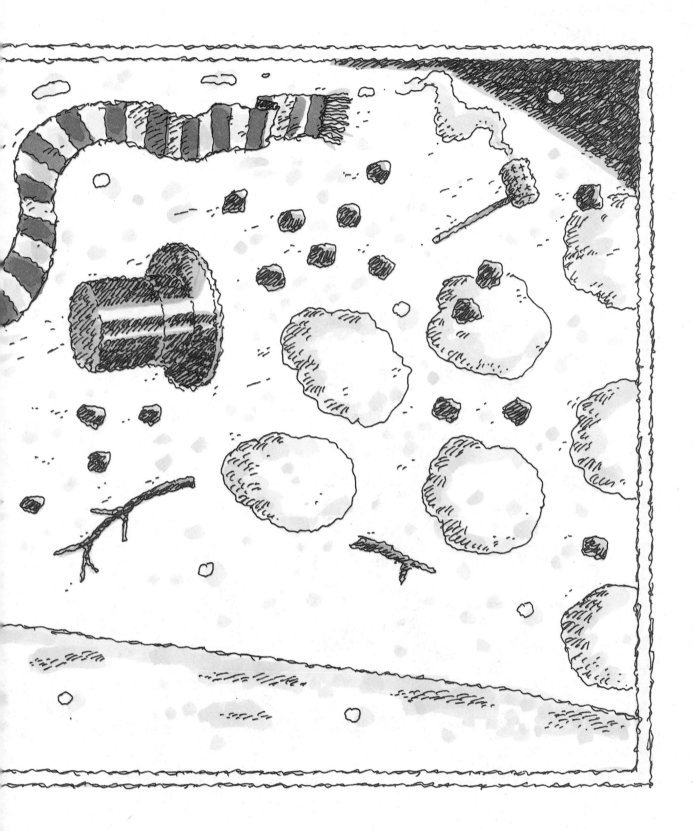

...a Snowman!